A Note to Parents and Caregivers:

*Read-it!* Readers are for children who are just starting on the amazing road to reading. These beautiful books support both the acquisition of reading skills and the love of books.

 The PURPLE LEVEL presents basic topics and objects using high frequency words and simple language patterns.

 The RED LEVEL presents familiar topics using common words and repeating sentence patterns.

 The BLUE LEVEL presents new ideas using a larger vocabulary and varied sentence structure.

 The YELLOW LEVEL presents more challenging ideas, a broad vocabulary, and wide variety in sentence structure.

 The GREEN LEVEL presents more complex ideas, an extended vocabulary range, and expanded language structures.

 The ORANGE LEVEL presents a wide range of ideas and concepts using challenging vocabulary and complex language structures.

When sharing a book with your child, read in short stretches, pausing often to talk about the pictures. Have your child turn the pages and point to the pictures and familiar words. And be sure to reread favorite stories or parts of stories.

There is no right or wrong way to share books with children. Find time to read with your child, and pass on the legacy of literacy.

Adria F. Klein, Ph.D.
Professor Emeritus
California State University
San Bernardino, California

Editor: Jill Kalz
Designer: Amy Muehlenhardt
Page Production: Brandie Shoemaker
Art Director: Nathan Gassman
Associate Managing Editor: Christianne Jones
The illustrations in this book were created with watercolor and pencil.

Picture Window Books
5115 Excelsior Boulevard
Suite 232
Minneapolis, MN 55416
877-845-8392
www.picturewindowbooks.com

Printed in the United States of America.

**Library of Congress Cataloging-in-Publication Data**
Klein, Adria F. (Adria Fay), 1947–
Max and the adoption day party / by Adria F. Klein ; illustrated by
Mernie Gallagher-Cole.
p. cm. — (Read-it! readers. The life of Max)
Summary: When his friend José has his adoption day party, Max brings him a
special present.
ISBN-13: 978-1-4048-3145-2 (library binding)
ISBN-10: 1-4048-3145-2 (library binding)
ISBN-13: 978-1-4048-3283-1 (paperback)
ISBN-10: 1-4048-3283-1 (paperback)
[1. Adoption—Fiction. 2. Parties—Fiction. 3. Friendship—Fiction. 4. Hispanic
Americans—Fiction.] I. Gallagher-Cole, Mernie, ill. II. Title.
PZ7.K678324Mad 2006
[E]—dc22                                              2006027269

# Max and the Adoption Day Party

## by Adria F. Klein
## illustrated by Mernie Gallagher-Cole

Special thanks to our advisers for their expertise:

Adria F. Klein, Ph.D.
Professor Emeritus, California State University
San Bernardino, California

Susan Kesselring, M.A.
Literacy Educator
Rosemount–Apple Valley–Eagan (Minnesota) School District

PICTURE WINDOW BOOKS
Minneapolis, Minnesota

Max and José are good friends.

José asks Max to come to his
adoption day party.

7

José tells Max that the party celebrates the day his mom and dad adopted him.

José calls the day his "gotcha day."

Max asks if there will be ice cream and cake.

José smiles and nods his head.

On Saturday, Max goes to José's apartment for the party. He brings a special present for José.

There are many friends at the party. José's mom and dad bring out the cake. It says "HAPPY ADOPTION DAY JOSÉ" in purple letters.

14

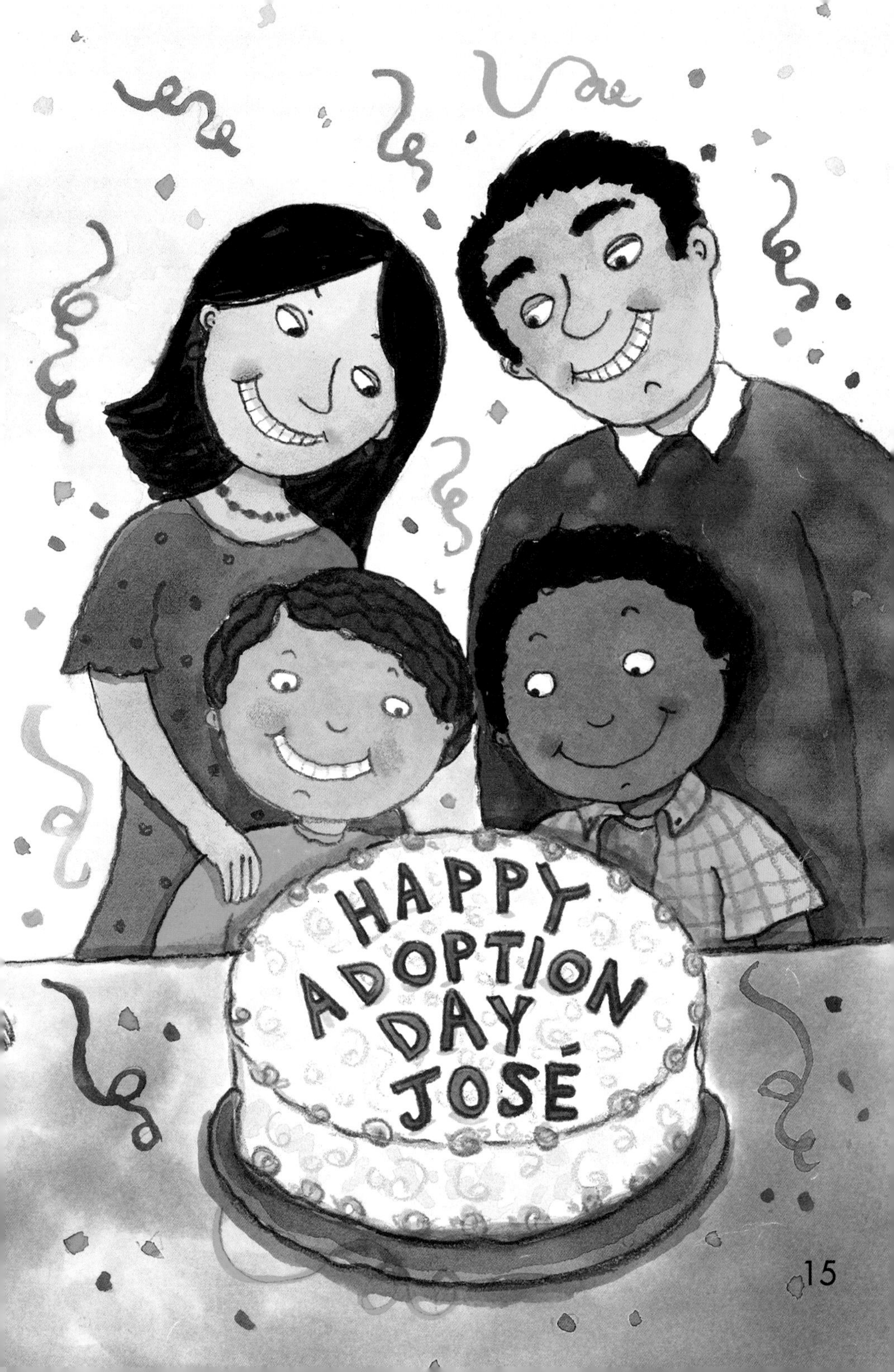
HAPPY
ADOPTION
DAY
JOSÉ

Max, José, and all of their friends eat chocolate cake and ice cream.

They go on a treasure hunt.

They pin the tail on the donkey.

José opens his presents. The present from Max is a soccer ball.

Max can't wait for José's adoption day party next year. Max and José are good friends.

# More *Read-it!* Readers

Bright pictures and fun stories help you practice your reading skills. Look for more books at your level.

*Max Celebrates Chinese New Year*
*Max Goes to a Cookout*
*Max Learns Sign Language*
*Max Stays Overnight*
*Max's Fun Day*

*Max Goes on the Bus*
*Max Goes Shopping*
*Max Goes to School*
*Max Goes to the Barber*
*Max Goes to the Dentist*
*Max Goes to the Library*

Looking for a specific title or level? A complete list of *Read-it!* Readers is available on our Web site:
**www.picturewindowbooks.com**